GEORGE
AND
MARTHA

written and illustrated by JAMES MARSHALL

HOUGHTON MIFFLIN COMPANY BOSTON

For George and Cecille

LIBRARY OF CONGRESS CATALOG CARD NUMBER 74-184250
ISBN 0-395-16619-5 (rnf.)
ISBN 0-395-19972-7 (pbk.)
PRINTED IN THE UNITED STATES OF AMERICA

Printed in the United States of America

Y 15 14 13

FIVE STORIES ABOUT TWO GREAT FRIENDS
STORY NUMBER ONE
SPLIT PEA SOUP

Martha was very fond of making split pea soup. Sometimes she made it all day long. Pots and pots of split pea soup.

Soup's
ON

If there was one thing that George was *not* fond of, it was split pea soup. As a matter of fact, George hated split pea soup more than anything else in the world. But it was so hard to tell Martha.

One day after George had eaten ten bowls of Martha's soup, he said to himself, "I just can't stand another bowl. Not even another spoonful."

So, while Martha was out in the kitchen, George carefully poured the rest of his soup into his loafers under the table. "Now she will think I have eaten it."

But Martha was watching from the kitchen.

"How do you expect to walk home with your loafers full of split pea soup?" she asked George.

"Oh dear," said George. "You saw me."

"And why didn't you tell me that you hate my split pea soup?"

"I didn't want to hurt your feelings," said George.

"That's silly," said Martha. "Friends should always tell each other the truth. As a matter of fact, I don't like split pea soup very much myself. I only like to make it. From now on, you'll never have to eat that awful soup again."

"What a relief!" George sighed.

"Would you like some chocolate chip cookies instead?" asked Martha.

"Oh, that would be lovely," said George.

"Then you shall have them," said his friend.

STORY NUMBER TWO
The Flying Machine

"I'm going to be the first of my species to fly!" said George.

"Then why aren't you flying?" asked Martha. "It seems to me that you are still on the ground."

"You are right," said George. "I don't seem to be going anywhere at all."

"Maybe the basket is too heavy," said Martha.

"Yes," said George, "I think you are right again. Maybe if I climb out, the basket will be lighter."

"Oh dear!" cried George. "Now what have I done? There goes my flying machine!"

"That's all right," said Martha. "I would rather have you down here with me."

The Tub
STORY NUMBER
THREE

George was fond of peeking in windows.

One day George peeked in on Martha.

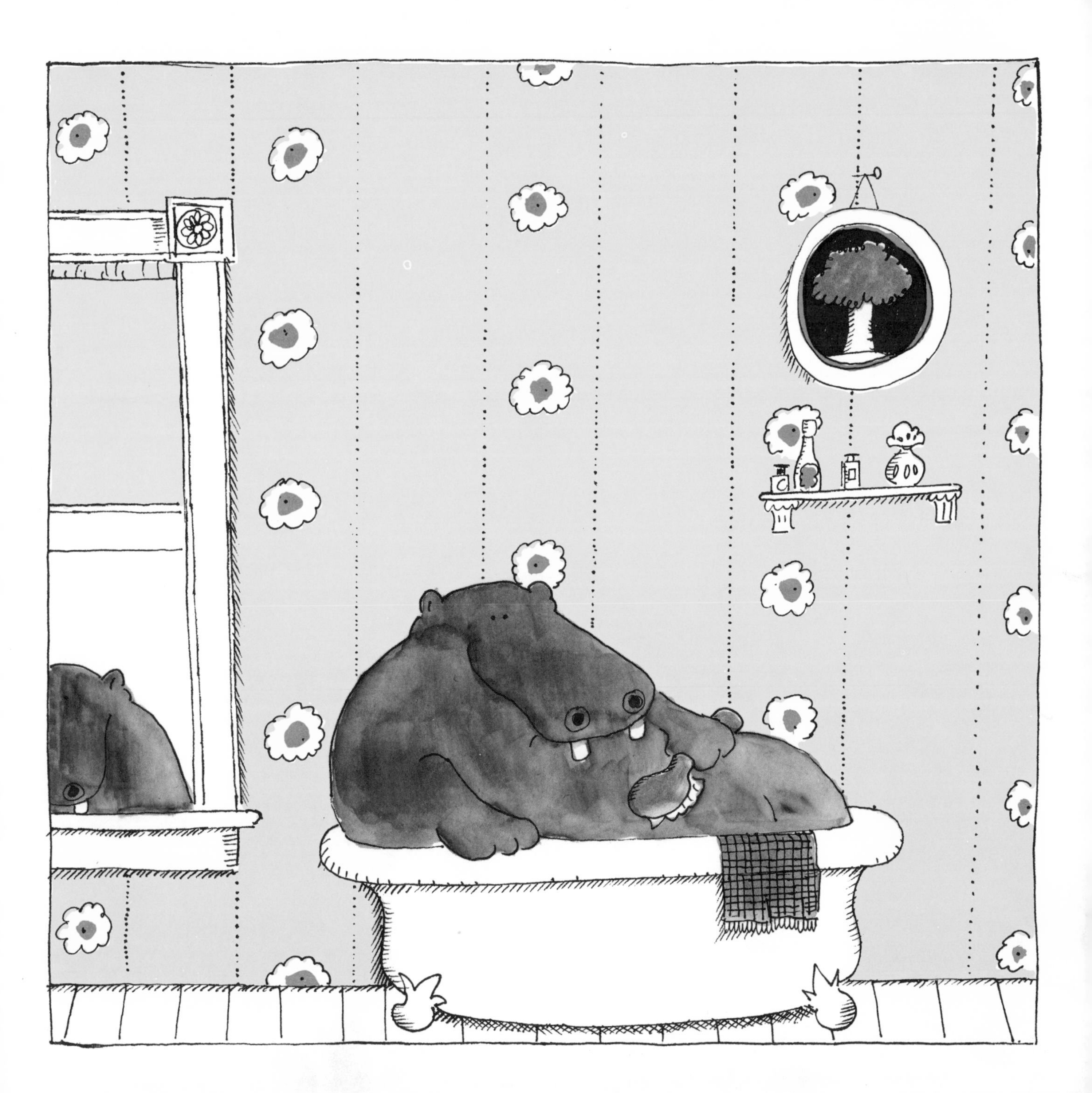

He never did *that* again.

"We are friends," said Martha. "But there is such a thing as privacy!"

STORY
NUMBER
FOUR
The Mirror

"How I love to look at myself in the mirror," said Martha.

Every chance she got, Martha looked at herself in the mirror.

Sometimes Martha even woke up during the night to look at herself.

"This is fun." She giggled.

But George was getting tired of watching Martha look at herself in the mirror.

One day George pasted a silly picture he had drawn of Martha onto the mirror.

What a scare it gave Martha. "Oh dear!" she cried. "What has happened to me?"

"That's what happens when you look at yourself too much in the mirror," said George.

"Then I won't do it ever again," said Martha.

And she didn't.

The Last Story
The Tooth

One day when George was skating to Martha's house, he tripped and fell. And he broke off his right front tooth. His favorite tooth too.

When he got to Martha's, George cried his eyes out.

"Oh dear me!" he cried. "I look so funny without my favorite tooth!"

"There, there," said Martha.

The next day George went to the dentist.

The dentist replaced George's missing tooth with a lovely gold one.

Buck
McTOOTH
D.D

When Martha saw George's lovely new golden tooth, she was very happy. "George!" she exclaimed. "You look so handsome and distinguished with your new tooth!"

And George was happy too. "That's what friends are for," he said. "They always look on the bright side and they always know how to cheer you up."

"But they also tell you the truth," said Martha with a smile.